The Spring Surprise

Based on *The Railway Series* by the Rev. W. Awdry

Illustrations by
Robin Davies

EGMONT

EGMONT

We bring stories to life

First published in Great Britain 2011
by Egmont UK Limited
239 Kensington High Street, London W8 6SA

Thomas the Tank Engine & Friends™

CREATED BY BRITT ALLCROFT

Based on the Railway Series by the Reverend W Awdry
© 2011 Gullane (Thomas) LLC. A HIT Entertainment company.
Thomas the Tank Engine & Friends and Thomas & Friends are trademarks of Gullane (Thomas) Limited.
Thomas the Tank Engine & Friends and Design is Reg. U.S. Pat. & Tm. Off.

HiT entertainment

ISBN 978 1 4052 5613 1
1 3 5 7 9 10 8 6 4 2
Printed in Italy

FSC
Mixed Sources
Product group from well-managed
forests and other controlled sources
Cert no. TT-COC-002332
www.fsc.org
© 1996 Forest Stewardship Council

Egmont is passionate about helping to preserve the world's remaining ancient forests.
We only use paper from legal and sustainable forest sources.

This book is made from paper certified by the Forestry Stewardship Council (FSC),
an organisation dedicated to promoting responsible management of forest resources.
For more information on the FSC, please visit www.fsc.org. To learn more about
Egmont's sustainable paper policy, please visit www.egmont.co.uk/ethical

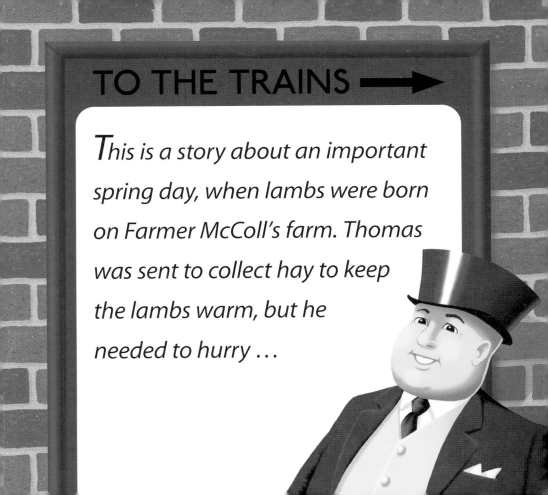

*T*his is a story about an important spring day, when lambs were born on Farmer McColl's farm. Thomas was sent to collect hay to keep the lambs warm, but he needed to hurry …

In the springtime, one of Thomas' favourite places on the Island of Sodor was Farmer McColl's sheep field. He liked to see the sheeps' smiling faces and to hear them call out when he passed.

"Baa! Baa!" the sheep would say.

And, "Peep! Peep!" Thomas would whistle back.

Thomas visited the field as often as he could.

One day, Thomas was passing the field when Farmer McColl waved to him. Thomas puffed to a stop.

"Hello, Thomas!" said Farmer McColl. "I'm glad you're here. I have some very special news. Some lambs are going to be born today."

Thomas was excited at the happy news. "I can't wait to meet them!" he peeped.

"Newborn lambs must have soft hay," Farmer McColl told him. "Can you go to the Old Barn at Maron to collect some?"

"Right away!" Thomas smiled, and he quickly chuffed away with his empty truck behind him.

On his way to Maron, Thomas thought about the lambs. "They will like the hay," he puffed, cheerfully. "But I wonder if there's anything else they would like?"

As Thomas passed the Bakery, he saw Percy waiting as his trucks were loaded with freshly baked bread. Thomas stopped to tell him about the lambs.

"How exciting!" peeped Percy. "I wish I could see the lambs, but I must deliver this bread."

An idea flew into Thomas' funnel. "Maybe the lambs would like some bread," he puffed. "May I have some?"

Percy agreed, and his crew quickly loaded a few trays of bread onto Thomas' truck. As Thomas steamed away, he was very pleased.

"I wonder what else the lambs might like?" Thomas wondered.

Soon, he saw James at the Garden Centre and told him about the lambs.

"I'd like to see them," chuffed James, "but I have to deliver these flowers to the Hospital."

Thomas was sure the lambs would enjoy the colourful spring flowers, too. "May I have some for the lambs?" he asked, and James agreed.

Before long, Thomas was nearly at Maron. As he approached the junction, he saw Charlie waiting at a signal.

"Hello, Charlie!" puffed Thomas. "I'm going to meet some newborn lambs today!"

"That sounds like fun," chuffed Charlie. "I have to collect cheese from the Dairy."

"Perhaps the lambs would like some cheese," said Thomas. "May I have some?"

Charlie agreed, and they went to the Dairy, where the cheese was loaded onto Thomas' truck.

Thomas hurried on to the Old Barn. A Farm Worker was waiting for him, along with stacks of hay bales.

He looked behind Thomas. "Your truck is full," he said. "There's no room for the hay."

"Fizzling fireboxes! I didn't think about that," Thomas worried. "I hope the lambs will like bread, cheese and flowers instead of hay."

When Thomas returned to the Farm, Farmer McColl was surprised that there was no hay in the truck.

"I thought the lambs would like these things more than hay," Thomas explained.

"No, Thomas." Farmer McColl looked cross. "The lambs must have hay to keep them warm. And they will be born before the sun goes down!"

Thomas felt very silly.

"I'm sorry," he wheezed. "I will leave these things here and collect the hay straight away!"

Thomas steamed back to Maron, saying over and over, *"I must get the hay, there can be no delay. The lambs will be born by the end of the day!"*

As he passed the Water Tower, Percy saw him and asked after the lambs.

"I'm sorry, Percy. I've no time to talk," Thomas answered, as he whooshed by.

He saw James at a Junction, then Charlie at a station. They wanted him to stop, but Thomas had to hurry on for the lambs.

It was getting late by the time Thomas arrived at the Old Barn.

"Hello again!" Thomas puffed to the Farm Worker. "Now I have plenty of room for the lambs' hay. Please will you load it on quickly? I must hurry, or the lambs will be cold," he added.

"Of course I will, Thomas!" the man smiled.

Once loaded up, Thomas headed back to Farmer McColl's farm. He was tired and thirsty, but he couldn't stop to rest or drink. The lambs would be born soon!

Thomas steamed so quickly, his axles ached. *"I must go fast, without delay. The lambs must have hay by the end of the day!"* he wheeshed.

At last, Thomas reached the farm. Was he too late?

"You're just in time," Farmer McColl said, running up with a smile. "I need that soft hay right away. The lambs have just been born!"

The Farmer brought the hay to the barn and opened the doors. Thomas was delighted to see the mother and her little lambs.

The next day, Thomas took some schoolchildren to visit the farm. He saw the little lambs snuggled up together in the warm hay.

Farmer McColl laid out the bread, cheese and flowers that Thomas had brought the day before, and the children enjoyed a splendid spring picnic.

"I have a surprise for you, Thomas," smiled Farmer McColl. "I named this lamb 'Thomas' . . . after you!"

"Peep! Peep!" Thomas whistled, happily.

And the lamb answered, "Baa! Baa!"

Win 1 of 10 Holiday Goody Bags!

We're giving away 10 Thomas Holiday Goody Bags, containing the Thomas Holiday Annual, the Thomas & Friends magazine, fun activity sheets and a Fisher-Price Take-n-Play™ Thomas at the Farm Playset – everything you need to keep your little one entertained over the spring holiday!

To enter simply hop online and count how many Easter eggs are hiding in the pages of the Thomas Story Library website! Get the answer right and you could be in with a chance of winning!

The number 1 destination for Thomas books!

visit www.mythomaslibrary.co.uk